The Cowboy Kid

by A.H. Benjamin and
Garyfallia Leftheri

W

First published in 2015 by
Franklin Watts
338 Euston Road
London
NW1 3BH

Franklin Watts Australia
Level 17/207 Kent Street
Sydney
NSW 2000

FSC
www.fsc.org
MIX
Paper from
responsible sources
FSC® C104740

A CIP catalogue record for this book is available
from the British Library.

ISBN 978 1 4451 3946 3 (hbk)
ISBN 978 1 4451 3949 4 pbk)
ISBN 978 1 4451 3948 7 (library ebook)
ISBN 978 1 4451 3947 0 (ebook)

Series Editor: Jackie Hamley
Series Advisor: Catherine Glavina
Serles Designer: Peter Scoulding

Printed in China

Franklin Watts is a divison of
Hachette Children's Books,
an Hachette UK company.
www.hachette.co.uk

Max wanted to be
a cowboy.

He got a lasso and started to practise.

He swung the lasso
over his head and …

Oops! He caught himself.

"You'll get better," smiled Mum.

Max aimed at the
gatepost and …

Oops! He caught the cat.

"Bad luck," said Dad.

Max aimed at a
flower pot and ...

Oops! He caught his uncle.

"Keep practising, Max!"
his uncle said.

Max decided to help his sister catch her puppy and …

Oops! He caught his sister.

"Max, no!" panted his sister.

"Will I ever be a cowboy?"
thought Max, sadly.

One day, Max went to a
country show with Dad.
He took his lasso
with him.

Suddenly, a big bull came charging towards them.

The gate to his field had been left wide open.

Max aimed his lasso at
the bull and …

25

Oops! He caught the gate. Max pulled hard and the gate closed just in time.

27

"Well done!" cried Dad.

"Three cheers for the Cowboy Kid" shouted everyone.

Puzzle 1

a

b

c

d

e

f

Put these pictures in the correct order.
Now tell the story in your own words.
Can you think of a different ending?

Puzzle 2

excited   dismayed

thrilled

annoyed   jolly

cross

Choose the words which best describe Max and which best describe his sister in the pictures. Can you think of any more?

Answers

Puzzle 1

The correct order is:

1e, 2c, 3a, 4f, 5b, 6d

Puzzle 2

Max   The correct words are excited, thrilled.
The incorrect word is dismayed.

Sister   The correct words are angry, cross.
The incorrect word is jolly.

Look out for more stories:

Mary and the Fairy
ISBN 978 0 7496 9142 4

The Bossy Cockerel
ISBN 978 0 7496 9141 7

Tim's Tent
ISBN 978 0 7496 7801 2

Sticky Vickie
ISBN 978 0 7496 7986 6

Handyman Doug
ISBN 978 0 7496 7987 3

Billy and the Wizard
ISBN 978 0 7496 7985 9

Sam's Spots
ISBN 978 0 7496 7984 2

Bill's Scary Backpack
ISBN 978 0 7496 9468 5

Bill's Silly Hat
ISBN 978 1 4451 1617 4

Little Joe's Boat Race
ISBN 978 0 7496 9467 8

Little Joe's Horse Race
ISBN 978 1 4451 1619 8

Felix and the Kitten
ISBN 978 0 7496 7988 0

Felix, Puss in Boots
ISBN 978 1 4451 1621 1

Cheeky Monkey's Big Race
ISBN 978 1 4451 1618 1

The Naughty Puppy
ISBN 978 0 7496 9145 5

Prickly Ballroom
ISBN 978 0 7496 9475 3

The Animals' Football Cup
ISBN 978 0 7496 9477 7

The Animals' Football Camp
ISBN 978 1 4451 1616 7

That Noise!
ISBN 978 0 7496 9479 1

The Wrong House
ISBN 978 0 7496 9480 7

The Frog Prince and the Kitten
ISBN 978 1 4451 1620 4

For details of all our titles go to: www.franklinwatts.co.uk